In My Pocket

Written by June Crebbin

Illustrated by Katharine McEwen

WALKER BOOKS

In my pocket
were ...

Two
stripy socks

Three
torn tickets

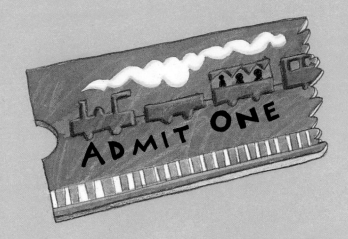

ADMIT ONE

CLUB CINEMA

SWIMMING CLUB — LEISURE CENTRE

Four
freckled frogs

Five
twisty twigs

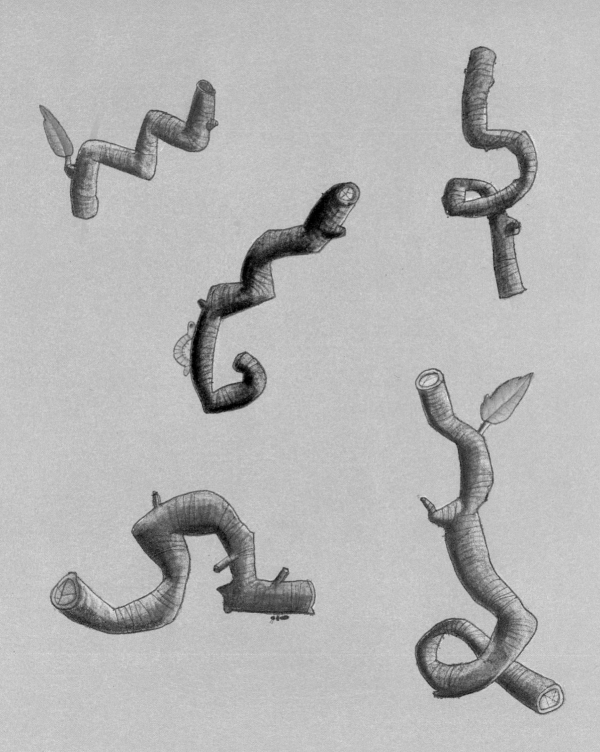

Six
tasty toffees

Seven
stickers for swops

Eight
clinking coins

Nine
coloured crayons

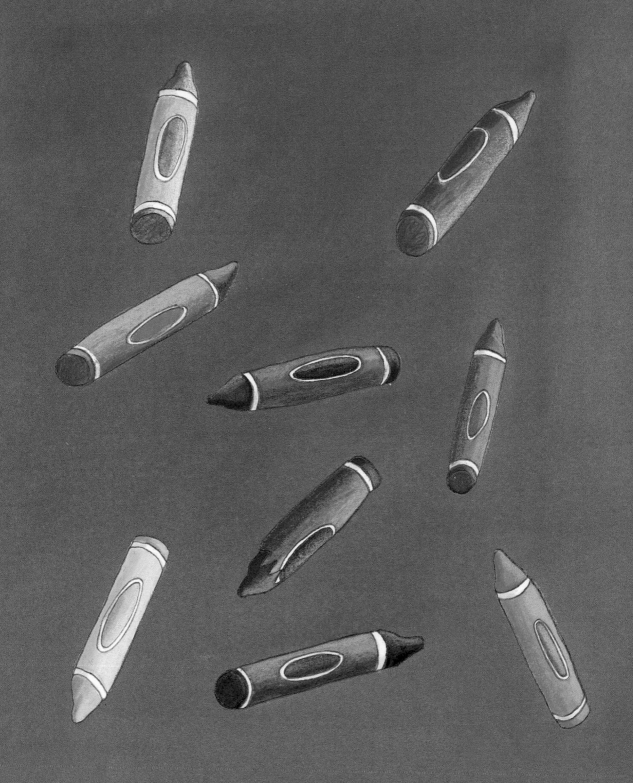

Ten
marvellous
marbles

and ...

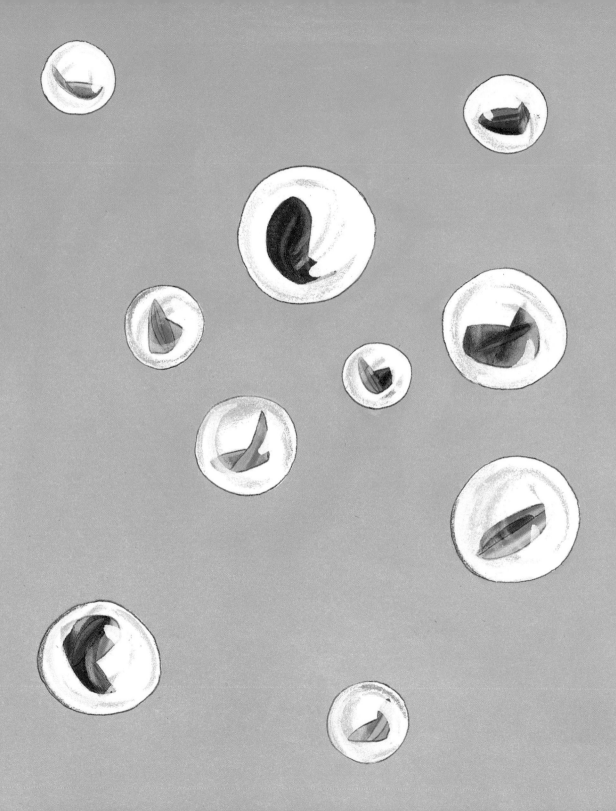

One
HUGE
hole!

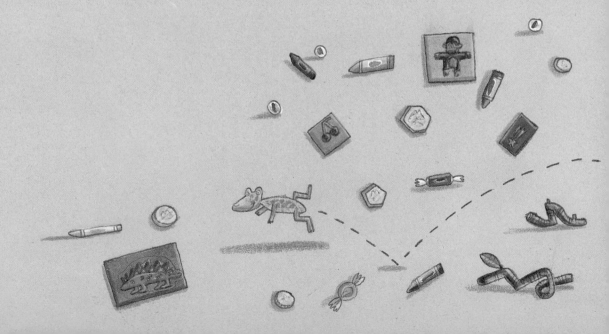

For Hannah and Lauren
J.C.
For Nick, my own pocket-dweller
K.McE.

First published 2001 by Walker Books Ltd
87 Vauxhall Walk, London SE11 5HJ

2 4 6 8 10 9 7 5 3

Text © 2001 June Crebbin
Illustrations © 2001 Katharine McEwen

This book has been typeset in Avant Garde

Printed in Hong Kong

British Library Cataloguing in Publication Data:
a catalogue record for this book
is available from the British Library

ISBN 0-7445-8306-3